To: Sydney,
I hope you always
have good friends
like Deedo and Dido.
Sandy Gardineer

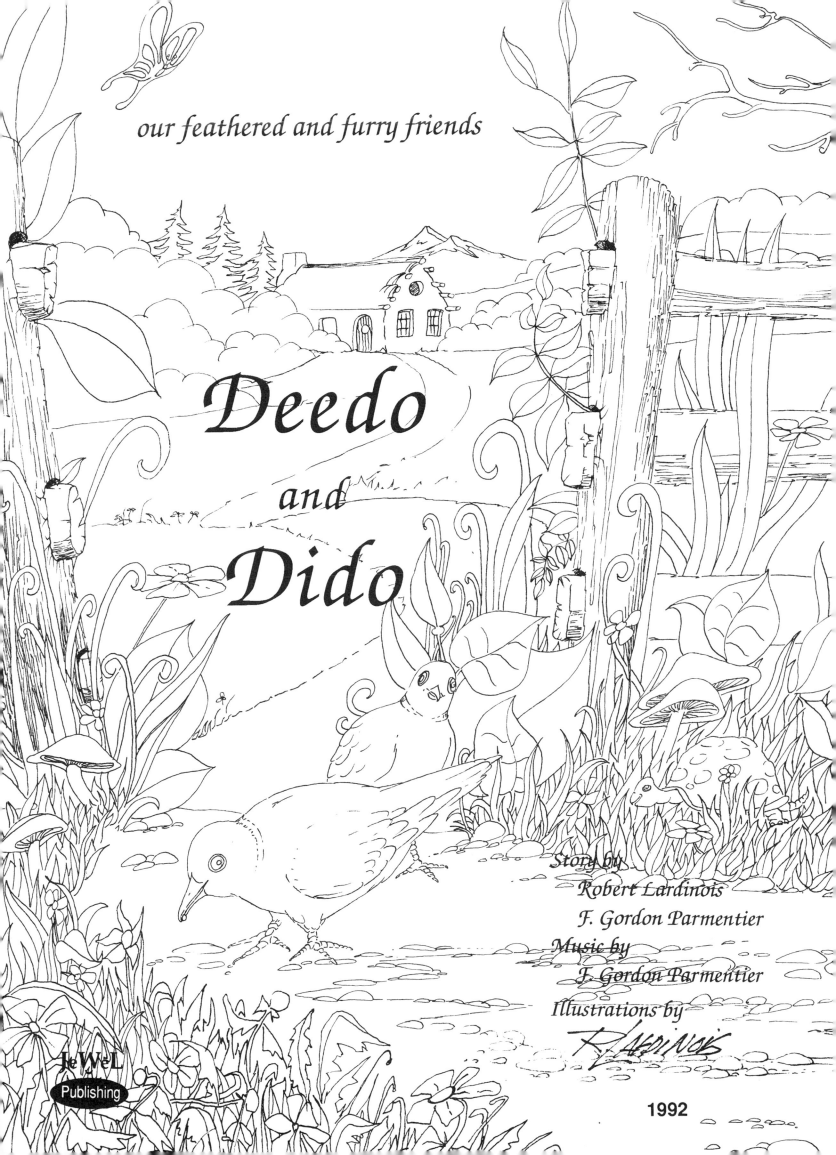

dedicated to

our feathered and furry friends

Library of Congress Cataloging in Publication Data

Lardinois, Robert & F. Gordon Parmentier. Deedo & Dido.

music by F. Gordon Parmentier; illustrations by Robert Lardinois;
edited by Sandy Lardinois.
p. cm. -- (Our feathered and furry friends)
Summary: Deedo and Dido, two orphaned doves, strive to help their new animal friends, a captive dog and three goldfish threatened by a hungry cat. Includes twelve songs.
[1. Doves--Fiction. 2. Animals--Fiction. 3. Friendship--Fiction. 4. Stories in rhyme. 5. Songs.]
I. Parmentier, F. Gordon. II. Lardinois, Sandy, 1946- . III. Title. IV. Series.
PZ8.3.L324De   1992 [E]--dc20 92-20879
ISBN: 0-9629715-1-0

Published in the United States by JeWeL Publishing, Denver

Printed in Stevens Point, WI by Worzalla

Verses that are songs are indicated by italicized print.
The rest of the songs immediately follow the story.

The Red House

F.G.Parmentier

In a small red house high— on— a hill lived a pot - ter,

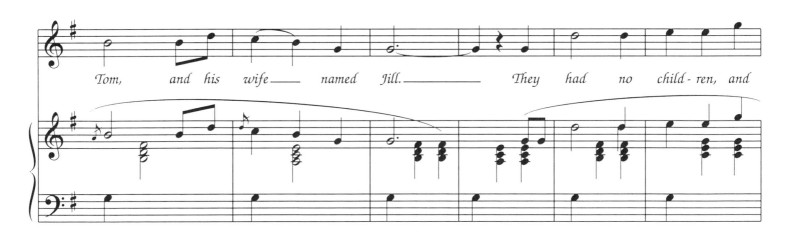

Tom, and his wife—— named Jill.—— They had no child - ren, and

times— were bad. A dog and two— doves— were all they had.—

In a small red house high on a hill
Lived a potter, Tom, and his wife named Jill.
They had no children, and the times were bad.
Two doves and a dog were all they had.

Kelly was a collie who liked to run;
He loved to play and have some fun.
The doves were a gift to Jill from Tom
To give her joy and sense of calm.

They named Joy, the lady dove
And, Prince, the boy, to share her love.
With straw from Jill, they built a nest;
And then they took their needed rest.

There soon appeared one egg, then two,
Mostly white with specks of blue.
Tiny beaks at last broke through--
One broke free, then there were two.

When the sun came out at break of day,
The mother dove just flew away
To seek a new life on her own,
And Prince was left to cope alone.

With broken heart he did his best
To feed the babies in the nest.
Prince grew weak as the babies fed.
And a few days later Prince was dead.

Jill fed them daily and by hand
'Til strength was gained and they could stand
What names for this sister and brother?
Deedo for one, Dido for the other.

One morning at the end of June
Just after summer's first full moon,
The time had come for them to try
To use their wings and start to fly.

Deedo was the first to fly;
She flew into a tree nearby.
Then Dido spread his wings and flew--
He landed on the potter's shoe.

The doves took flight both far and near;
They soared the skies without much fear
And landed in an apple tree;
It was a perch with much to see.

A great white dog was tied below,
Her eyes were sad and full of woe.
"Who are you," said Deedo, the dove,
"And why so sad?" she cooed from above.

The dog looked up with her long white face.
"Simone's my name--I'm stuck in this place.
I chased the piglets and the hens
And jumped into the lambing pens.

"I often tend to be quite bad,
But being tied here makes me sad.
I wish I could be running free
Like the dog next door who doesn't like me."

"Oh, Kelly is our family pet.
It's a shame you two have never met.
It's our mistress that he really loves.
'Tis true," agreed the little doves.

"We must be off to fly some more
But we live real close, just next door.
We'll be back to see if we
Can find a way to set you free."

The doves flew off to a nearby pond,
Three goldfish swam in the depths beyond.
They had big eyes and tails with fans--
Orange and white and shades of tans.

Up above, on a lilac bush,
Deedo gave Dido a gentle push,
"I wonder, with their enormous size,
When do they ever close their eyes?"

The fish responded, "We don't sleep.
A constant vigil we must keep.
We're glad to be in our little pool--
Except for a cat, who can be cruel.

"Every night 'bout six or seven,
A very nasty cat named Kevin
Comes stalking us throughout the night
And gives us just an awful fright."

"Poor little fish!" the doves replied,
"Your peaceful rest has been denied.
All we've met have a trouble or two;
We want to help, we really do.

"Right now it's time for us to fly,
But we'll be back in the wink of an eye.
Perhaps we'll find a plan that may
Keep Kevin Cat out of the way."

Back they flew to the potter's house
And found their cage--sshhh--like a mouse.
DEEDO and DIDO started to doze
When a plan appeared to ease their woes.

If they could work Simone's release,
She would have to help make peace
Between the cat and the goldfish three,
So they could live in harmony.

Simone agreed to help chase Kevin
Knowing freedom would be like heaven.
The two little doves started to peck
At the rope around the big dog's neck.

DEEDO and DIDO worked all the day
Pecked through the rope, but not all the way.
"We will return to complete this task;
Just be patient, that's all we ask."

The doves flew homeward as darkness fell.
Simone was happy and anxious as well;
The very next day she'd be free at last--
She would run far, she would run fast.

She'd rid the fish of Kevin Cat;
It should not take long to handle that.
Too happy to sleep inside her shed,
She curled beneath the tree instead.

Later that night when all was still,
Kevin crept 'round to make his kill.
Still as a rock, the sly cat waited;
He knew a fish for lunch was fated.

That Kevin was near, the fish could sense;
The fish were nervous; the cat was tense.
Close and closer, with cat claws bare,
A sudden WHO-O-O-T soon filled the air!

Kevin the fright'ner was frightened instead,
The hoot so close that Kevin fled.
He ran and he ran--faster than fast;
It was Simone he finally ran past.

Kevin dashed into the shed for Simone.
His heart beat fast, he let out a groan.
The big, old owl so frightened the cat,
He couldn't stop shaking after all that.

Simone awakened with a start;
It didn't take long to do her part.
She slammed the door of the wooden shed
Where, on most nights, she made her bed.

"Eek!" screamed Kevin, and his hair stood high,
"I am trapped, and I'm going to die."
"Aha!" said Simone as she looked at him,
"Now you will pay for your life of sin.

"There is a way to change your mood--
Three days and nights without your food.
Then we will talk about your fate,
If, by then, it is not too late!"

When the sun came up at the break of day,
Simone saw the doves from where she lay.
She nodded her head toward the door,
"Kevin will bother the fish no more!"

DEEDO and DIDO peeked through a hole,
And saw poor Kevin, as black as coal.
The doves worked hard 'til it was done;
Simone was finally free to run.

"I'm free! I'm free! At last I'm free!
No one will ever capture me."
Then off she ran through fields and streams,
And off through the woods as in her dreams.

On she ran in a happy mood
'Til hunger made her think of food.
Then she thought of her big blue bowl
Awaiting her on her grassy knoll.

Simone looked out but had lost her way;
She had been running for most of the day.
The creeks and meadows all looked the same:
Simone was lost, and who's to blame?

Back in the shed, Kevin Cat was scared;
His confidence had been impaired.
The doves stopped by and wondered where
Simone had gone--she should be there!

"Simone is gone and has not been back.
How many days? I can't keep track.
I'm locked in here," the cat then said,
"No food or water, I'm almost dead.

"It's natural for cats to feast on fish,
But I will try to respect your wish.
I will leave them alone, no doubt.
Just please find a way to let me out!"

DEEDO and DIDO glanced at the latch.
It didn't take long to release the catch.
Kevin crawled out and wasn't so rude
After he drank and ate some food.

They figured Simone had lost her way,
And vowed to find her that very day.
Although she'd wanted to be free,
Home was, by far, the place to be.

The cat offered his help to find her;
They all could try to be much kinder.
DEEDO told Kelly about their plan;
He knew the way that most dogs ran.

The four set out to search for Simone.
Kelly's first find was an old dog bone.
The doves flew high and circled wide;
Kevin looked sharply from side to side.

Kelly's nose sniffed the trail of Simone;
Then Kevin spied a tail by a stone
Way up a hillside under a tree.
The doves flew swiftly, anxious to see.

The animals hurried to the site
And found Simone, who awoke in fright.
When she saw her friends, she nearly cried.
"I'm glad you found me--I might have died.

"*Please help me find my way back home;*
I know I never more will roam.
Just be my friends and visit me
When I am tied to the apple tree."

They all agreed to be her friend,
And Kevin forgave her in the end.
They went home where her bowl was filled;
She ate without a morsel spilled.

* * *

The friends came by to see Simone;
And sometimes Kelly shared a bone.
The doves would perch in the apple tree
And coo a simple melody.

And Kevin did not stalk the fish
Although it was his dearest wish.
He thought and thought and thought of that--
For, after all, he's still a cat!

Songs

Abandoned

F.G.Parmentier

#2   Slow and softly

When the sun came out at break of day, the
moth - er dove just flew a - way to seek a new life on her own,——
—— and Prince was left—— to cope a - lone.

Simone

F.G.Parmentier

#3   Moderate

"Si-mone's my name -- I'm stuck in this place. I chased the pig-lets and the hens and

jumped in-to the lamb-ing pens. I of-ten tend to be quite bad, but

be-ing tied here makes me sad. I wish I could be run-ning free!"

Fish Speak

F.G.Parmentier

"Ev-'ry night 'bout six or sev'n, a ve-ry nas-ty cat named Kev'n comes

stalk-ing through the night and gives us an aw-ful fright."

Kevin Cat Stalks

F.G.Parmentier

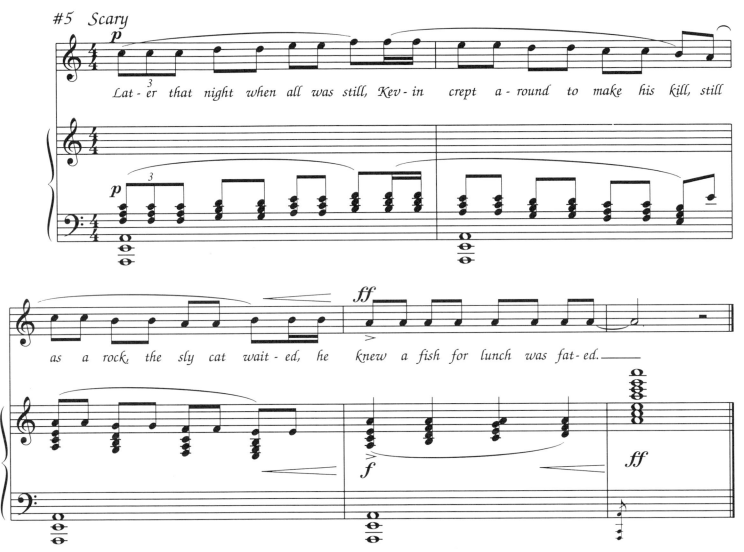

Later that night when all was still, Kev-in crept a-round to make his kill, still as a rock, the sly cat wait-ed, he knew a fish for lunch was fat-ed.

Frightened

F.G. Parmentier

Lyrics:

Kev - in the fright - 'ner was fright - ened in-stead, the hoot so close that Ke - vin fled. He ran and he ran just fast - er than fast; it was Si - mone that he fin - 'lly ran past!

Kevin Pays

F.G.Parmentier

"Eek!"screamed Kev-in, and his hair stood high, "I am trapped, and I'm go-ing to die."

"A-ha!" said Si-mone as she looked at him. "Now you'll pay for your life of sin!"

I'm Free

F.G.Parmentier

Simone Lost

F.G.Parmentier

#9   Moderate, sadly

Si - mone— looked but she had lost her way; She had been run - ning for'

most of the day.   The   creeks   and   mead - ows   all

looked   the   same   Si - mone was lost, and   who's to   blame?

"Let Me-ow'"

F.G.Parmentier

"It's nat-'ral for cats to feast on fish, but I will try to re-spect your wish.

I will leave them a - lone, no doubt. Just find a way to let me - ow', ME-OW'!"

Please Help

F.G.Parmentier

#11 A bit sad, moderate

"Please help me find my way back home; I know I nev - er

more will roam. Just be my friends and vis - it me when I am tied to the

ap - ple tree."

Happy Friends

F.G.Parmentier

#12 Fast and happy

The friends came by to see— Si-mone; and some-times Kel - ly shared a bone. The

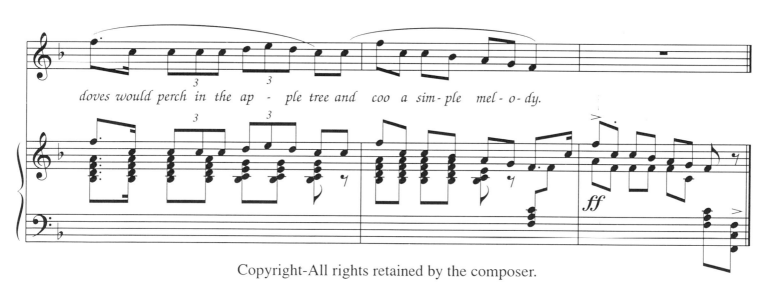

doves would perch in the ap - ple tree and coo a sim-ple mel-o-dy.

To order the following:

- cassette tape ($9.95 + $2.50 s & h)
  music on one side;
  music with vocals on other

- unabridged story and additional song, *"Mr. Dove"* ($2.50)

contact: **JeWeL** Publishing
P.O. Box 36006
Lakewood, CO 80236-6006

Prices available
through 1992

About the Artist

Robert J. Lardinois, born in Green Bay, Wisconsin, studied at the Layton School of Art in Milwaukee and the Chicago Academy of Fine Arts. His works are in many private collections throughout the U.S. and abroad, and he shares his techniques in art classes at various institutes and art organizations. His color techniques range from brilliant to obscure; his landscapes evoke realism, impressionism, and abstractionism. An environmental theme is currently the focus of works recycling various plastics and paper with sand and clay to create relief sculpture wall pieces. Robert's home along the Little Wolf River abounds with the animals, birds, and nature that he loves.

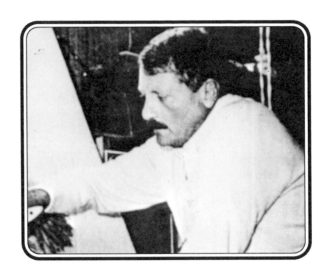

Robert J. Lardinois

About the Composer

F. Gordon Parmentier

Born in Green Bay, Wisconsin, F. Gordon Parmentier earned his Master's degree from the Paris Conservatory of Music in 1952. Moving to California the next year, he taught at Mills College and in the University of California extension system. During a thirteen-year residency on the coast, he had works performed by the San Francisco, Vancouver, and Indianapolis Symphonies. A one-act opera was also produced in San Francisco. Returning to Wisconsin, Parmentier taught in the Green Bay public schools and at UWGB. His music has also been performed in Europe by the Wisconsin Youth Symphony and the Green Bay Symphony.